# RIGHT-WAY ROUND AND UPSIDE DOWN

The Story of Henry and Amy

For
Brother Dave
(Sandy &
Imogen)
and
Sister Mel
(Tyrone)

Miranda and
Charlotte,
(Mandy
& Pam)

Mark
and Liz,
(Hannah)

Trish
and Tani

Scholastic Children's Books,
Commonwealth House, 1-19 New Oxford Street,
London WC1A 1NU, UK
a division of Scholastic Ltd

London ~ New York ~ Toronto ~ Sydney ~ Auckland
Mexico City ~ New Delhi ~ Hong Kong

First published as *Henry and Amy* by Scholastic Australia Pty Limited, 1998
This edition published in the UK by Scholastic Ltd, 2000

Text and illustrations copyright © Stephen Michael King, 1998

ISBN 0 439 01352 6

Printed in Hong Kong

RIGHT-WAY ROUND
AND UPSIDE DOWN

The Story of Henry and Amy

Stephen Michael King

Hippo

E very time Henry tried
to draw a straight line . . .

it

turned

out

wiggly.

2

When everyone around him looked up . . .

Henry
looked
down.

3

If he thought it was going
to be a beautiful sunny day . . .

it would rain.

Splish

Splash

Sploosh

6

**E**arly one morning when Henry
was out walking backwards,
trying very hard to walk forwards,

he bumped into Amy.

Amy could do everything right.

She *never* tied her shoe laces together

or buttered the wrong side of her toast.

She always remembered her umbrella

and could write her very own name.

Henry thought everything Amy did was amazing.

So Amy showed him his **right** from his **left**,

his front from his back,

and that the sky was up
and the ground was down.

One day they decided
to build a treehouse.

Amy worked on a plan so that
it would sit in the tree just right.

Henry added lots of squiggly wiggly
bits that made them both giggle.

 Deep down, Amy wished everything she did wasn't so perfect.

So Henry found
her a coat and a hat
that didn't match.

Then he taught Amy
back-to-front

and
topsy turvy.

They rolled down a hill sideways . . .

and together they learnt
how to fly paper aeroplanes.

Henry and Amy are the very, very best of friends . . .

right-way-round

and upside down.